DISNEP's
Flubber
A Special Collector's Edition

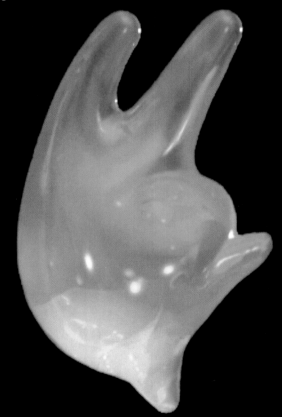

Adapted by Lucy Dahl
Based on the motion picture from Walt Disney Pictures
Screenplay by John Hughes and Bill Walsh
Produced by John Hughes and Ricardo Mestres
Directed by Les Mayfield

DISNEP PRESS
New York

ACKNOWLEDGMENTS

Many people have been extraordinarily helpful to me while writing and collecting information for this book, and I would like to thank each and every one of them:

Robin Williams, Marsha Williams, Marcia Gay Harden, Ted Levine, Clancy Brown, Christopher McDonald, John Hughes, Les Mayfield, Ricardo Mestres, David Nicksay, Louise Spencer, Hero Naritas, Kathy Breen, Philip Alexy, Scott Leberecht, Roni McKinley, Amanda Montgomery, Teri Avanian, Steve Sonn, Holly Clark, Mary Reardon, Laura Schultz, Peter Crosman, Chris Cundy, Chris Capp, Michael Umble, Phil Bray, Deardra Morrison, John LaViolette, Tracey Jones, and my editor, Erin McCormack.

Unit photography by Phil Bray.

Printed in the United States of America.

First Edition

1 3 5 7 9 10 8 6 4 2

Library of Congress Catalog Card Number: 97-80129

ISBN: 0-7868-3149-9 (trade)
ISBN: 0-7868-5061-2 (lib. bdg.)

FOR TRACEY

one inches wide

six inches compact at the center

four microthrusters

one-inch
rounded edge

I am **Weebo**.

video
camera

Polaroid camera

six-inch color video screen

air brakes

4

NAME: WEEBO

AGE: SEVENTEEN

SEX: FEMALE

HOBBIES: FLYING

INTERESTS: SCIENCE

FRIENDS: WEBBER, FLUBBER, THE PROFESSOR

BEST FRIEND: THE PROFESSOR!

FAVORITE FOOD: KNOWLEDGE!

FAVORITE COLOR: YELLOW

BEST ASSET: MEMORY

WORST DEFECT: JEALOUSY

I am a flying computer. . . .

com•put•er \kəm-'pyü-tər\ *n.* a programmable electronic device that can store, retrieve, and process data.

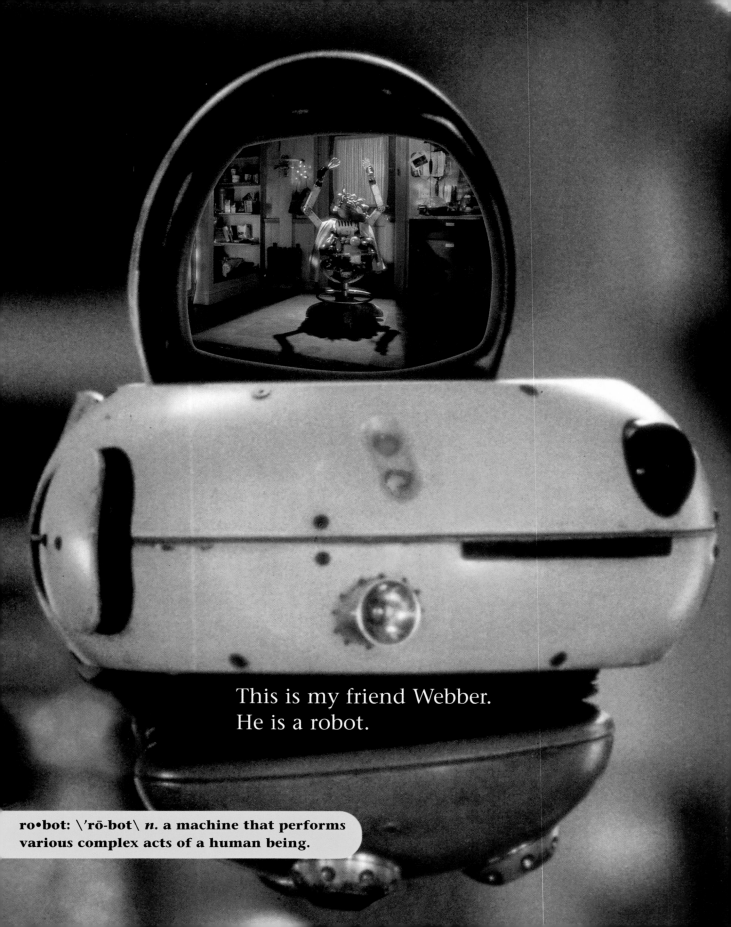

This is my friend Webber.
He is a robot.

ro•bot: \'rō-bot\ *n.* a machine that performs
various complex acts of a human being.

And this is my Professor.

pro•fes•sor \pre-ʹfes-er\ *n.* a faculty member of the high-
est academic rank at an institution of higher education.

He is a teacher, with such a big brain . . . really big . . . so **BIG** that his last name is Brainard!!

brain \brān\ *n.* the organ of thought.

-ard \erd\ *n. suffix* characterized by possessing an excessive quality.

A human being's brain is 90 percent of the head. It weighs three pounds. A human only uses 10 percent of the brain, but I think my Professor uses a different 10 percent than most other people!

That is why he is so clever. . . .

clev•er \'kle-ver\ *adj.* mentally quick and resourceful but often lacking in depth and soundness.

My calculations are always precise. . . . This particular calculation:

BRAIN + ARD x CLEVER = PROFESSOR

is most interesting, as it proves to me that only computers are perfect! Because even if a human is brainy, he might still lack depth and soundness, at least in some areas!

That is why the Professor needs me, WEEBO.

Ten inches deep at the center and my sound is crystal clear.

Not to mention my memory . . . An elephant is said to have the greatest capacity for memorization and can actually remember *almost* everything, but I, WEEBO, remember everything! I store it all in my hard drive. I even remember how I was made!

hard drive \härd drīv\ *n.* a computer accessory that is used to hold software programs and computer files.

MOVIE SECRETS

These are my concept design sketches.

Twelve different WEEBOs were made for the filming.
Me with regular wiring,
Me with a flashbulb,
Me with an electric plug,
Me with a Polaroid camera,
Me broken,
Me dying,
And six shells without
    any insides for the fight scenes.

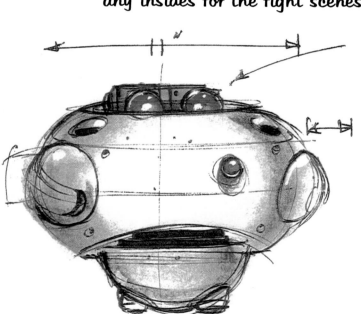

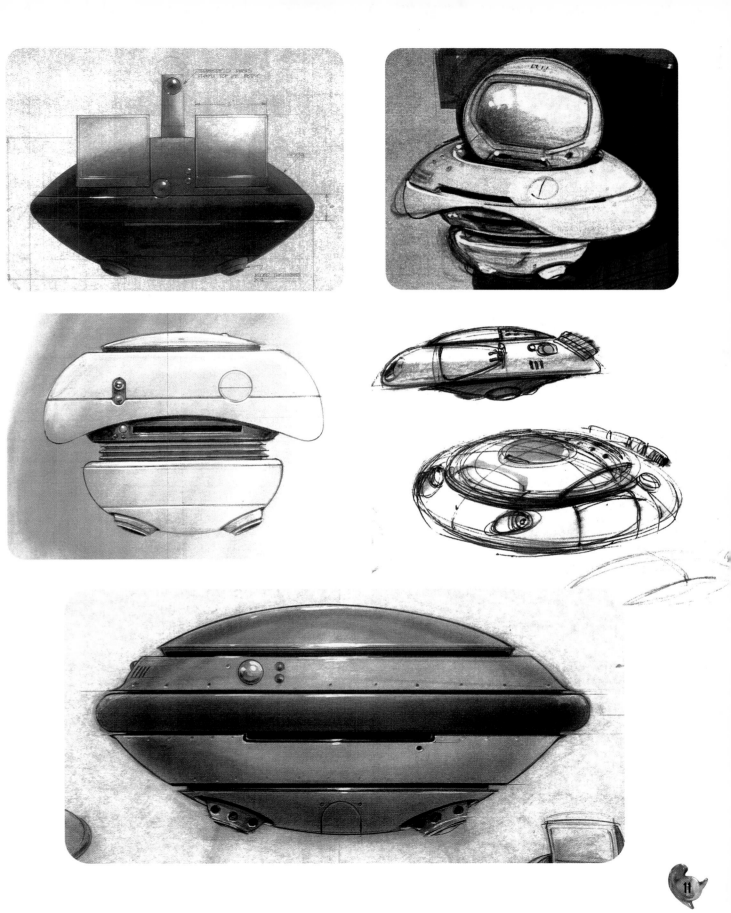

I am operated by remote control, which is operated by three humans.

My flaps open and close by pushing buttons.

My eye and my screen are connected to foot pedals.

My body is attached to a steady arm that later is removed by CGI (computer graphic imaging), which gives the illusion that I'm floating.

The Professor also made Webber.
Webber cooks and cleans for us. . . .

NAME: WEBBER

AGE: SEVEN

SEX: MALE

HOBBIES: COOKING

INTERESTS: TV

FRIENDS: WEEBO, THE PROFESSOR, SARA

BEST ASSET: KIND

WORST DEFECT: CLUMSY

MOVIE SECRETS

Here are Webber's concept designs:
He, too, is operated by three people. . . .
One to operate his overall movement.
One to operate his arms.
One to operate his body.

All these motions are
    remotely controlled.

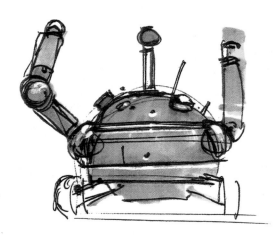

This is our house:

Let me show you around. Almost everything in our house has some scientific meaning. We have blackboards in every room, because the Professor never knows when he is going to have a clever idea, and when he does, he has to write it down immediately. Otherwise, it is forgotten!

Plants are a very important part of the Professor's experiments.

We use potatoes as batteries for our clocks.

Some might describe our house as messy and disorganized, but I think it is a neat mess!!

It is a particular day of a particular month in a particular year when this story begins. . . .

Webber is preparing breakfast for the Professor.

Did you know that an egg cooks at 149 degrees Fahrenheit?

egg + butter + heat = a fried egg

Or that a coffee bean is crushed with pressure ten times its weight?

Scientific Fact

The human body temperature stays at about 98.6 degrees Fahrenheit. Heat in the Professor's body is generated by food, cooked by Webber! But at the same time heat is always being lost. There are two ways to prevent the heat from escaping. One is to dress appropriately. . . .

The other is for the body to prevent heat from escaping by shutting off blood vessels near the skin and making the hair stand on end.

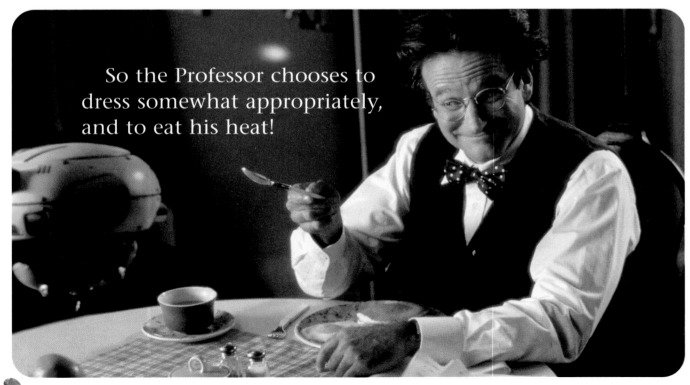

So the Professor chooses to dress somewhat appropriately, and to eat his heat!

I remember everything the Professor remembers, and I remember everything the Professor forgets. I never forget to remember, unless I remember to forget, and then if the Professor forgets, all is forgotten!!

So I remember to do for the Professor what he forgets to do for himself.

CLASSES
LUNCH
FACULTY MEETING
CLASSES

Our schedule is rather similar every day.
Except every now and then . . .

6:30 P.M. MARRIAGE TO SARA JEAN REYNOLDS

I remember everything!

I check my dictionary file. . . .

mar•riage \'mar-ij\ *n.* an intimate or close union.

I am faced with human malfunction.

mal•func•tion \mal-'funk-shen\ *vi.* to fail to operate in the normal or usual manner.

I do not want the Professor to have an intimate or close union with Sara Jean Reynolds.

I just want Webber and me to take care of him.

He made us just the way he wanted us to be—perfect. There is no such thing as a perfect human being!!!!

I have to do something. I *must* do something. The Professor *can't* marry Sara.

I didn't exactly *forget* to remind the Professor to remember. I just remembered to forget to leave the schedule on my screen for very long. Just like last time when he forgot to get married!

And the time before that!

Each time he forgets, water comes out of her eyes, and she becomes very angry. She just doesn't understand him the way I do.

One day, the Professor said, "I love her."

I didn't understand this human word, so I looked in my dictionary file and chose the meaning that I thought best suited the description of Sara Jean Reynolds.

love \luv\ *n.* a score of zero (as in tennis).

Sara Jean Reynolds = love (a score of zero)

Then I found the definition that best fits my meaning for the Professor.

in love \in luv\ *adj. phr.* inspired by affection.

That's me!! WEEBO, inspired by affection for the Professor. My hard drive runs for him . . . everything is him! I live for him, work for him, fly for him! All of my inspiration is my Absentminded Professor. He inspires me. I inspire him. I am in love!!!!

Of course, the Professor is also inspired by his scientific experiments, and I am one of those!

That very afternoon at approximately 6:30 P.M., Sara waited at the church.

This was the score:

LOVE Sara . . .
. . . ADVANTAGE WEEBO!
(another tennis term!)

We can't be blamed for forgetting to remember about the wedding after all. We were inspired! The Professor was working away, busy with a new sparkling, sizzling fluid. It was boiling in the mixing tank. . . .

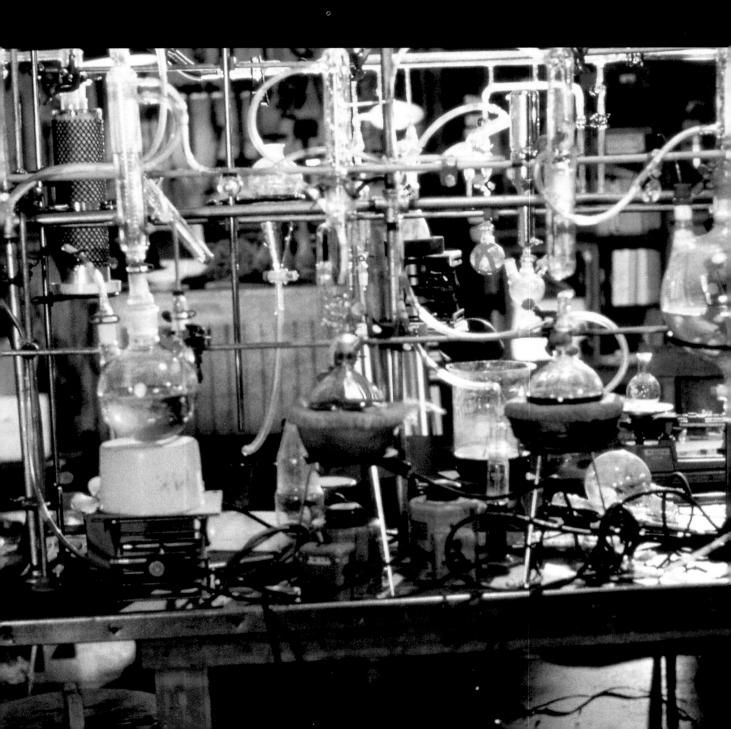

He added a hair from his head . . . turned up the heat . . . sealed the lid . . . plunged in a little energy . . .

When the Professor mixed the ingredients, he transferred his energy (breakfast + lunch = heat) to the ingredients in the reaction chamber.

The substance absorbed the energy from the Professor and the heat from the reaction chamber.

But as the Professor pushed the plunger, it tickled the compound, releasing the already absorbed energy and **EXPLODING** out of the tank.

Scientific Fact
To tickle means to perturb.

per•turb \per-'terb\ *vt.* to throw into confusion.

Too bad . . . another blow up!

But then we heard a snuffle and a puff and a huff and a moan, a gurgle and a groan and a burp!

The mixing tank rose from the ground. . . .

I *can't* look. . . .

I *must* look. . . .

There was something inside this tank.

Something very powerful. Something *alive!*

Carefully, the Professor opened the lid. . . .

MOVIE SECRETS

The Flubber tank was levitated by wires that were attached to the sides and then later erased by a computer.

The Professor gasped. A green glow reflected from his face, and he gently reached into the tank with a smile.

A limy, slimy, rubbery, flubbery, wiggly, jiggly creature climbed onto the Professor's hand.

YUCK!

I couldn't believe my eye!

It *was* alive! No brain, no face, no screen, no hard drive, not even a floppy disk, just a rubbery, flubbery, floppy body that was *alive*!

The Professor was excitedly delighted!!

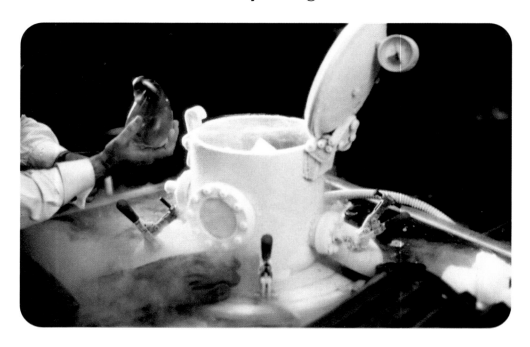

MOVIE SECRETS

All of the scenes with Flubber were filmed without any Flubber being used! Robin Williams, who plays the Professor, had to act as if Flubber was a real object, when really there was nothing there at all! Now *that's* acting!!

Months later, when the live-action filming was complete, the Flubber was added by CGI.

MORE MOVIE SECRETS
FLUBBER FACTS OF LIFE

Flubber is drawn on a computer and later added to the scenes.

1. The basic Flubber is made up of approximately twelve wire-frame balls, which are used for animating the Flubber.

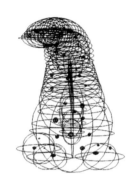

2. A wire mesh surface is drawn onto the spheres, giving a three-dimensional effect.

3. A plastic image is painted onto the mesh.

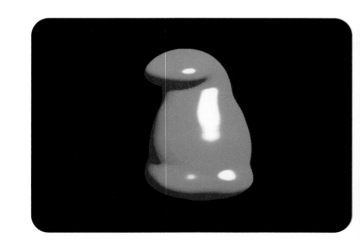

4. The background is then painted onto the plastic, giving the illusion of transparency and warping. Color shading and reflections are added to each frame.

The image is then transferred from the computer to film.

Each movement that Flubber makes has to be drawn, colored, animated, lit, shaded, and reflected for every frame. This takes a very long time and a great deal of skill.

The Flubber was created by a team of animators at Industrial Light and Magic in San Francisco, California.

Here is some of the concept art that was used to create Flubber's personality.

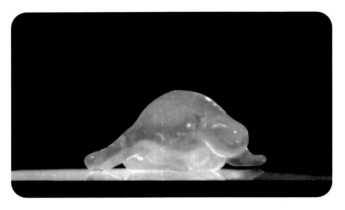

Despair

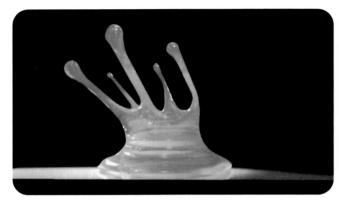

Shock

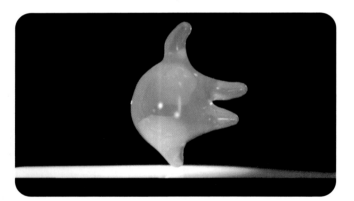

Dancing

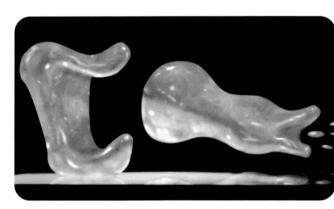

Sneezing

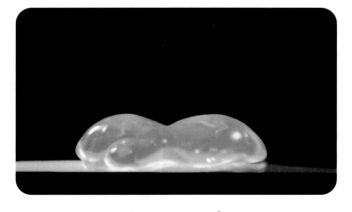

Depressed

Startled

32

Joy

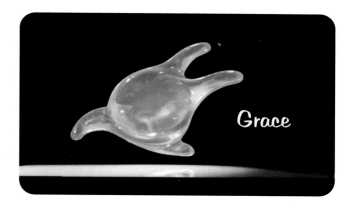

Grace

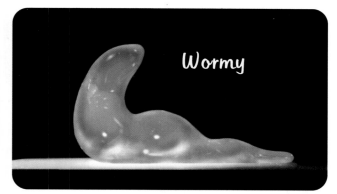

Wormy

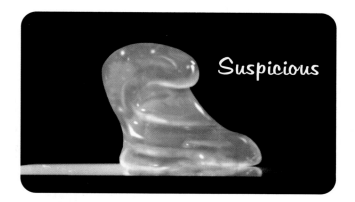

Suspicious

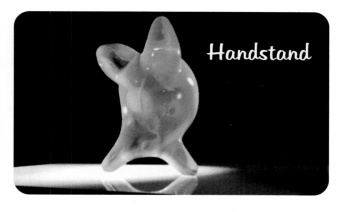

Handstand

Horrified

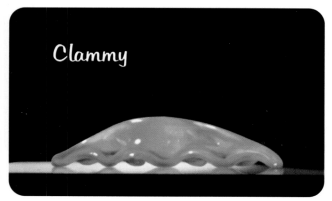

Clammy

Spooky

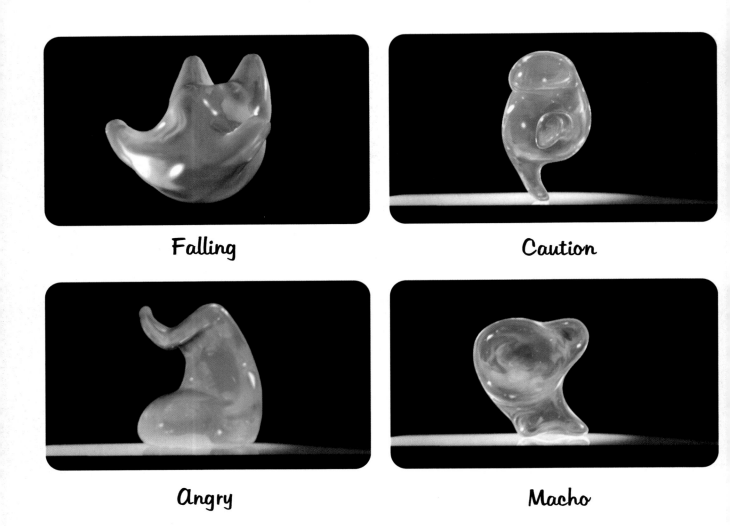

Falling

Caution

Angry

Macho

You might think that since I'm so jealous of Sara, I would be jealous of Flubber, too, because he means so much to the Professor. Well, I'm not. Flubber is not a threat to me in any way. He is a boy! That helps! I am much more beautiful, intelligent, entertaining, and charming than this hyperactive mass of molecules. Furthermore, my communication skills combined with my abilities, not to mention my sense of humor and intelligence, are far superior to our new family addition.

Scientific Fact

Flubber is a ⟨1⟩ *superconducting* ⟨2⟩ *polymer.* He is a ⟨3⟩ *superfluid* with ⟨4⟩ *Buckyballs* inside, holding internal energy levels that are arranged such that there are many ⟨5⟩ *metastable* states.

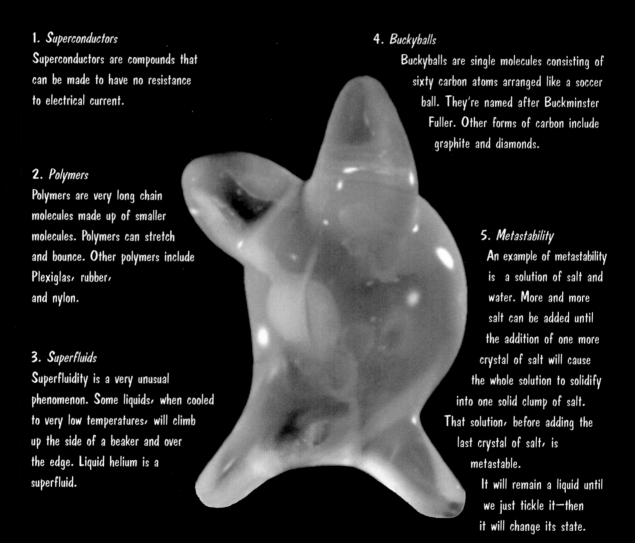

1. Superconductors
Superconductors are compounds that can be made to have no resistance to electrical current.

2. Polymers
Polymers are very long chain molecules made up of smaller molecules. Polymers can stretch and bounce. Other polymers include Plexiglas, rubber, and nylon.

3. Superfluids
Superfluidity is a very unusual phenomenon. Some liquids, when cooled to very low temperatures, will climb up the side of a beaker and over the edge. Liquid helium is a superfluid.

4. Buckyballs
Buckyballs are single molecules consisting of sixty carbon atoms arranged like a soccer ball. They're named after Buckminster Fuller. Other forms of carbon include graphite and diamonds.

5. Metastability
An example of metastability is a solution of salt and water. More and more salt can be added until the addition of one more crystal of salt will cause the whole solution to solidify into one solid clump of salt. That solution, before adding the last crystal of salt, is metastable.
It will remain a liquid until we just tickle it—then it will change its state.

Flubber's internal energy is stored in metastable states. The slightest noise or bounce triggers the release of Flubber's energy by jiggling his atoms and setting off a reaction.

The Professor is so excited!!

He asked me to take a photograph of the new addition to our family. But when my flash went off . . .

Flubber panicked—releasing his energy and jiggling his atoms!

SMASH!!

CRASH!!

WHAM!!

Once he starts, he doesn't stop!! He bounces faster and faster and flies higher and higher!!!

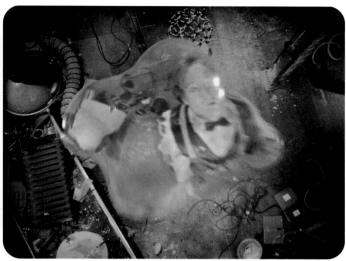

And he's gone!!

MOVIE SECRETS

During this scene, there was no Flubber. Robin Williams, the Professor, had to duck and dart at absolutely nothing in a perfectly silent, still lab!

Flubber was added later, by CGI.

The Professor had invented the world's first–ever flying rubber! A remark-able achievement.

I have only seen him this happy once before. The day I was made!

Everything was perfect. The Professor was bursting with happiness, and so was I. We had a new addition to our family, and it was not Sara Jean Reynolds!!

It was 6:30 A.M.! He had missed his wedding again!

Tee Hee!!

Sara was crying. Water was pouring out of her eyes, as if she had a leaking battery.

And I had my Professor all to myself again! But that very same day, the Professor cleaned himself up and went to Sara's office. He knew that he needed an exceptionally good excuse, so he took Flubber with him to help explain why he forgot the wedding—*again!!*

His plan was to explain to Sara that he missed the wedding because he was inventing Flubber! It was a new type of energy to sell to raise money to help Medfield, Sara's college.

But Sara was furious! She didn't want anything to do with him.

The Professor knew that if he could just explain his new invention, she would understand completely and forgive him—then everything would be back to normal.

The sight of Flubber only made the situation worse. She was outraged that the Professor missed their wedding because he was home playing with green goo!!

In his desperation, the Professor placed Flubber into his back pocket, opened the window, and tilted backward—falling from Sara's third-story office window!

The Professor expected Flubber to bounce him back up into Sara's office unharmed!

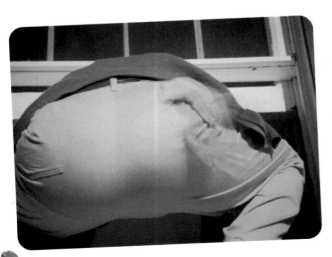

But Flubber is mischievous, and as the Professor jumped out of the window, Flubber flew out of his trousers!!

Scientific Fact
What goes down doesn't always come back up!

Sara slammed the window as more water trickled out of her eyes, and the Professor went away brokenhearted.

bro•ken•heart•ed \'brō•ken-'hart-ed\ *adj.* overcome with grief or despair.

MOVIE SECRETS

When Robin Williams fell out of the window, the drop was only three feet, and he landed on a mattress below.

I have never, *ever* hurt the Professor like that! He didn't actually forget the wedding. He just forgot to remember! He knew all about the wedding. She needs to get her battery fixed, so that it will stop leaking out of her eyes. Then maybe she might get her facts right.

When the Professor came home, I was waiting to console him.

But the plot thickens. . . .

This is Smith, and this is Wesson.

HOENICKER

cor•rupt \ke-'rupt\ *adj*. dishonest.

Both men work for Hoenicker, who is a very rich man.

Hoenicker's son attends Medfield, Sara's school, and Hoenicker has offered the school a lot of money on the condition that his son is given good grades.

That is a bribe.

To bribe is against the law—not a physics law, but a human law.

All three men are corrupt bad guys. . . .

. . . And the Professor is an honest good guy. Whichever way you formulate it—three wrongs do not, and will never, make a right.

The Professor, being honest and a little absentminded, failed Bennett (Hoenicker's son) in science. An F in science means Bennett gets kicked off the basketball team.

Hoenicker was angry and ordered Smith and Wesson to find out about the Professor.

bribe \brīb\ *n*. money or favor promised or given to a person in a position of trust to influence his judgment or conduct.

Later that day, everything was running smoothly at home. Webber was in the kitchen. . . .

And the Professor was outside squirting liquid Flubber on a golf ball and on the ground!

Smith and Wesson peeked through the window of the basement.

Then they crept around the side of the house to look into the kitchen window.

Little droplets of liquid Flubber were still on the ground from the golf ball experiment, and . . . they got

FLUBBERED!!

Even though Flubber defies all laws of physics, Smith and Wesson don't.

What goes up . . .

. . . must come down!!

. . . And down they came!
Away they went—well and truly Flubberized!!

MOVIE SECRETS

Two stuntmen dressed as Smith and Wesson acted the crash landing. Stuntmen and stuntwomen are professionally trained to fall onto hard surfaces without getting hurt.

Unaware of the commotion, Professor Brainard had a brain wave!

He was inspired.

A Flubber flight over Sara's house!

What a hu-man will do to attract a hu-woman!

Well, if the Professor is willing to risk his hard drive, so am I. I don't want to go, but the Professor needs me, so I will go.

I saw our lives flash right before my screen. . . .

And up we went. . . .

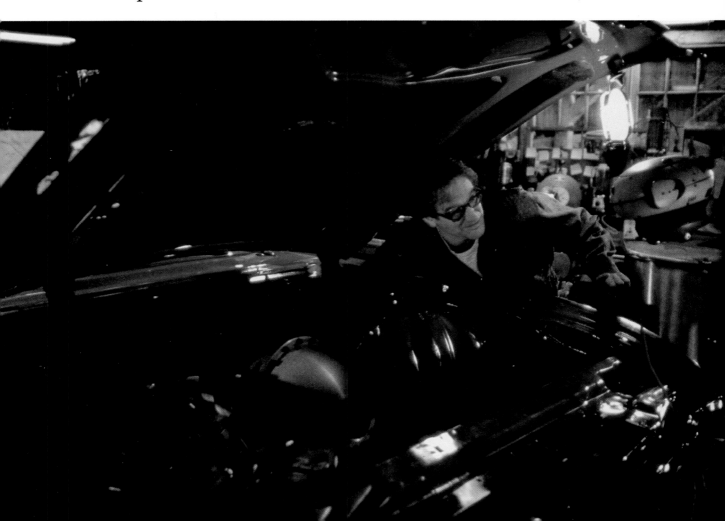

MOVIE SECRETS

The Flubberized flying car was filmed in many different ways.

A real car with a floating background in a studio was used for the close-up talking scenes.

A real car on a pivot in a studio was used for the close-up action scenes.

To give an accurate illusion of flying over the town, and for the wider angle shots, a model car on a pivot was created, compiled in three stages.

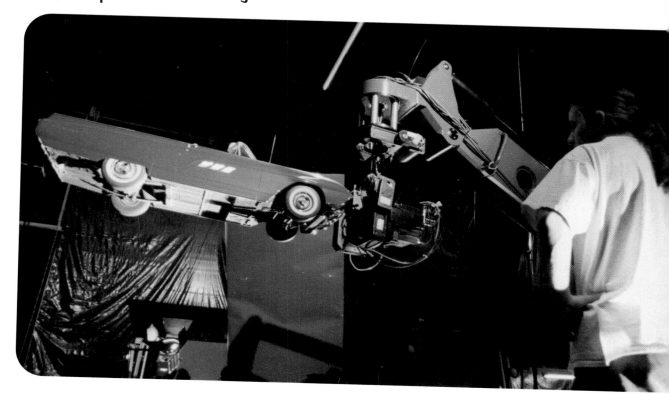

1. The model car was electronically moved in very slow increments.

2. A model of the town where the Professor lives was built and filmed from different angles.

3. Model clouds made of cotton wool on a wire frame were filmed in front of a painted skyline.

4. All three of these film plates were merged together, creating the Flubberized flying car scenes.

A week of filming produced about sixty seconds of final footage.

When we arrived at Sara's house, the unsuspecting Professor did not expect to see what he saw. . . .

Wilson, the Professor's arch enemy, was making his way into Sara's life, house, porch, and everything else! The Professor was outraged!

Sara, love. . . . Advantage, WEEBO!!

We flew home. Safe and sound, nice and cozy— just me and my Professor!

Later that evening, at Hoenicker's mansion, Smith and Wesson were trying to explain the unexplainable to their boss.

At last Sara was out of the picture . . . off the screen! Now everything could get back to normal function.

But the Professor was brokenhearted. I was jealous. I wanted the Professor to be in love with me!!!! I tried to cheer him up, but he told me it was a human problem.

A human problem?

Well then, *I* will become a human!!

When the Professor was asleep, I began the hologram human creation.

Now let's see— blue eyes, brown hair, soft . . . gentle . . . a little bit sexy—yes! Perfect! He's sure to fall in love with *me*!

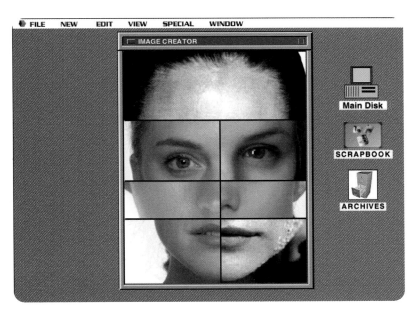

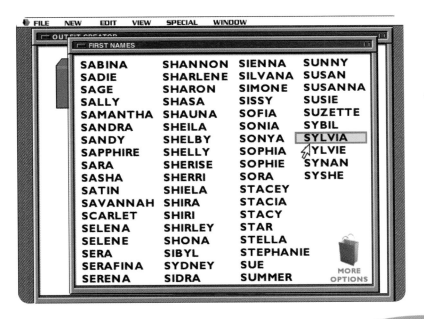

I think I'll call myself . . .

Sylvia.

MOViE SECRETS

The scene with Sylvia was filmed with a real woman. She was made transparent with computer imaging.

WOW!

This is really cool. Every dream has a Sylvia lining!!

Um . . . well, just as I was about to kiss the Professor . . .

. . . he woke up!!!!

kiss \kis\ *vt.* to touch with the lips esp. as a mark of affection.

I'm off . . .

I quickly plugged myself into the wall and pretended to be asleep.

ZZZZZZZZZZZZZZZZZ

I think Sylvia must have stimulated the Professor's hard drive, disrupting his usual sleep patterns and causing him to wake up suddenly and have a brainstorm!!!!

Then I realized that his sudden bright idea was about winning Sara's heart . . . again. Okay, it *is* a good idea to spray liquid Flubber onto tacks and pin the tacks into sneakers, thus giving Medfield the advantage in the basketball game against their rival, Rutland—Professor Wilson's school. But when will he notice ME?

brain•storm \ˈbrān-storm\ *n.* a sudden bright idea.

Off he went to the gym in the middle of the night to test his new idea.

At the gym, the Professor tied a rope to his ankle. The rope was attached to a heavy bag of sand. Then he sprayed liquid Flubber onto the bottoms of his shoes.

MOVIE SECRETS

A full-size gym was built inside an old abandoned Navy shipyard in San Francisco, California. A real gym could not be used, because the ceilings wouldn't be high enough to accommodate the lights, cranes, and flying rigs that were needed.

One jump
and he
was up . . .
and down.

The Flubber was on his sneakers, not his bottom, so instead of bouncing back up he landed with a bump!

The second jump was much more successful, . . .

. . . and the third, even more so, . . .

. . . flying in true Flubber fashion.

MOVIE SECRETS

Robin Williams, the Professor, was strapped into a harness underneath his sweatshirt. Cables were connected from the harness to a crane. The crane hoisted him up and down, giving the illusion of jumping.

First he practiced on a trampoline.

Then he moved on to the hard gym floor. The crane hoisted him up and down—from six feet to sixty feet in the air. Each jump was different. All together, the Professor jumped 1,240 times in one week!

While the Professor was out, I thought I might introduce myself to Flubber.

Webber unscrewed the tank. . . .

And the blobby mass began to speak FLUBBERISH. . . .

I could not find the translation of this particular language in my hard drive, so I recorded (REC.) the sound and duplicated (DUP.) the noise, imitating every whir.

Seeing his reflection in my lens, Flubber got scared and went berserk, . . .

"OOPS!"

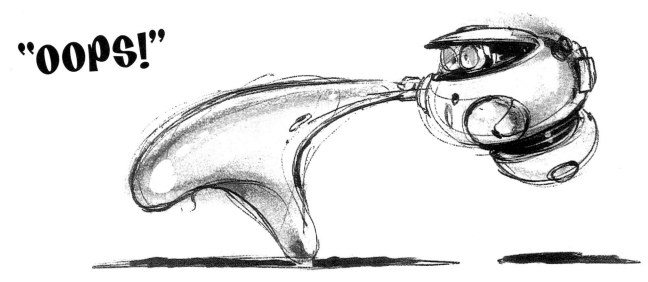

. . . bouncing all over the lab, . . . picking up energy on every bounce—smashing into test tubes and Bunsen burners, shattering glass, scattering papers, smacking into walls, bouncing off the ceiling and up the stairs. . . .

Thanks to my infrared scan, I found Flubber hiding in a cigar box.

Flubber was easy to find. He is full of hot energy! I coaxed him out, . . .

Scientific Fact
Infrared waves are invisible. They travel at the speed of light and are emitted by all warm objects.

MOVIE SECRETS

WEEBO was filmed in this scene alone, and later the Flubber was added by CGI.

. . . AND THE PARTY BEGAN!!!

Webber was rolling about, and Flubber was doing the mambo!!

When the Professor's away, the gadgets play!

I like to flop my floppy disks!

FUN . . .

64

FUN . . .

FUN!!!

The next day, the Professor went to the big game. There was nothing I could do about this. He didn't program the time into my disk! I couldn't forget to remind him, and he remembered to not forget. I hoped she was still mad at him.

Sara and Wilson sat together. The Professor sat behind them.

RUTLAND COLLEGE VS. MEDFIELD COLLEGE.

At halftime, the Professor crept into the locker room of Medfield and carefully poked one tack into each sneaker of the team members.

And then he returned to his seat.

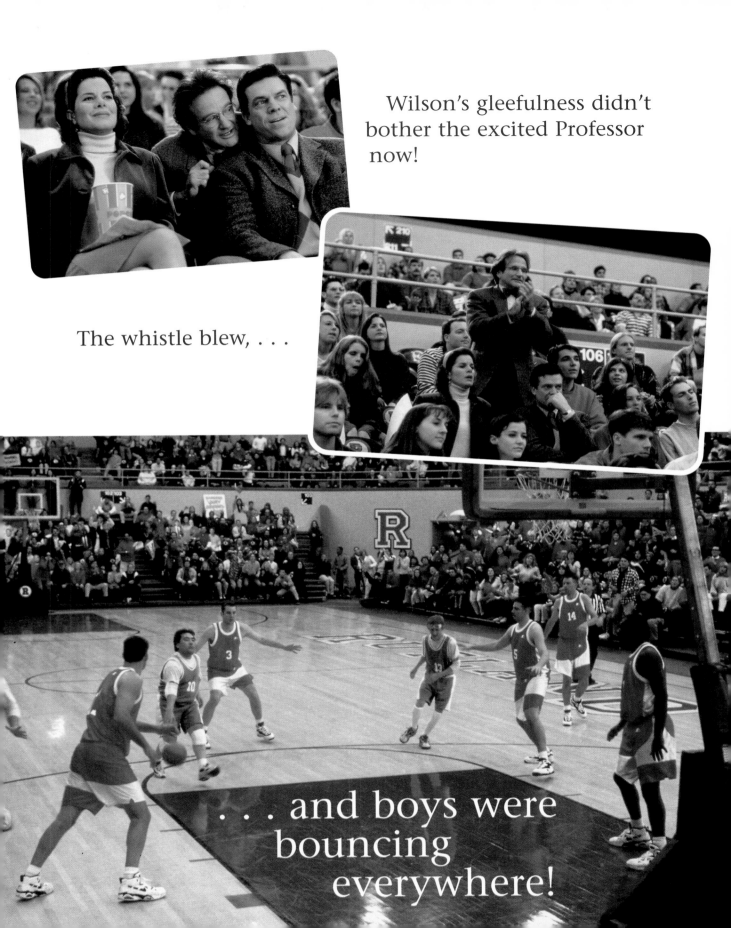

Wilson's gleefulness didn't bother the excited Professor now!

The whistle blew, . . .

. . . and boys were bouncing everywhere!

Nowhere in the rule book does it say anything about jumping too high!!

Rutland passed to Medfield, Medfield got it back, Rutland took a rotten shot, and Medfield's got its tacks!!

MOVIE SECRETS

Filming the basketball game took three weeks. The crowd consisted of 400 extras, and the players were actors who had to practice flying for a week before filming began. Wires were connected to harnesses that were under their shirts, and later the wires were erased by computer.

Medfield won!!

HOME | PERIOD | GUEST
00:00
68
RUTLAND
POSS
BONUS
70
MEDFIELD

Now all the Professor had to do was convince Sara that it was he who had helped her school win.

But Sara was still annoyed with the Professor and didn't believe him.

She got into Wilson's car and the new couple drove away. The Professor was miserable. He despised Wilson. Stealing his scientific ideas was bad enough, but now he was stealing his girlfriend, too.

As he flew home, he couldn't think of anything but Sara. He wasn't happy about the game. He didn't notice the beautiful night sky, and he didn't notice Hoenicker's car below.

But Hoenicker noticed the Professor. He certainly noticed the flying T-bird, and he wanted it!

At first when I saw the Professor I was pleased. I knew that Sara had rejected him. But as he came closer, I saw that this was serious!

My Professor was in a really bad way. He looked completely defeated, as if all his batteries were dead.

MOVIE SECRET

Three 1965 Thunderbird cars were used to film the special effects of flying.

He needed recharging, but what could I do? I can't plug him in. I can't restore his hard drive. I can't install a new program. I can't even give him a hug! I cannot help him, because he is human and I am not. That must be why he wants Sara so much. She *is* human, after all! It was then I realized that he didn't want me and he didn't want Sylvia. He wanted Sara. . . .

Suddenly I had a surge.

As the Professor spoke to me, I recorded every word.

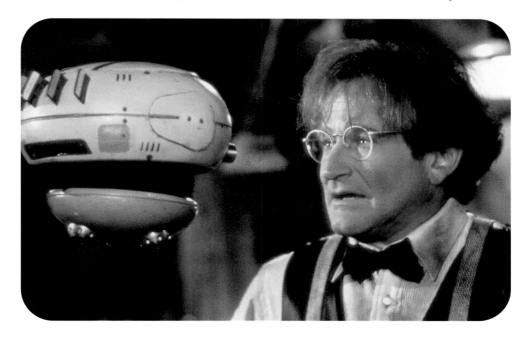

". . . the truth, Weebo, is that I am not absentminded because I'm crazy or inconsiderate or selfish. I'm absent-minded because I'm in love with Sara. Good night, Weebo, sleep tight."

In love!!

Why didn't he *say* so?

I flew over to Sara's house with the recording of the Professor's love speech.

She was sound asleep.

It is not polite to wake someone up, but this was important. I had to help my Professor.

I played the footage of my Professor confessing his love for her.

More water came leaking out of her eyes, but now she was smiling!

She went right over to our house and kissed him—while he was asleep!!

She must have rebooted his hard drive, because he woke up immediately! My Professor was overjoyed to see her, and he excitedly explained everything about Flubber and the game! *This* time, she believed him!

It was the middle of the night, and he took her for a joyride in the Flubberized car!

She can replace me in that car any time!

LOVEBIRDS IN A T-BIRD!

MOVIE SECRETS

This scene was filmed in a studio. The car was on a simulator. The night sky was a painted backdrop, and the clouds were created with 15,000 pounds of dry ice that was swirled about with fans.

The Professor was *in* love! *In*spired with *in*tense *in*timacy, *in*volving *in*forming Sara of his new *in*vention.

Sara was thrilled about Flubber as she realized the importance of this new substance for the planet. It was the solution to raising money and saving her school!

The Professor just wanted another kiss!

As they flew back toward home, neither of them noticed the big black Mercedes parked a few doors down from the house.

Love is blind!

Hoenicker and his men were waiting in the garage.

Hoenicker wanted to buy Flubber, but the Professor refused to sell it.

As Hoenicker and his men angrily drove away, I searched my hard drive for the name of an old student of the Professor, who presently works at an aerospace center.

The Professor told us that they would return the next day, and the happy new couple flew away—in search of Walter Beeker.

My Professor was happy, and *I* was happy that *he* was happy!

I was tired and went to sleep early.

Suddenly, there was a bang. I woke up with a jolt. It took a moment for me to boot up, but when I did, this is what I saw. . . .

Smith and Wesson had broken into our house! They had a flashlight and a club.

They were after Flubber.

I had to stop them. I quietly followed them down to the basement. Poor Flubber was terrified and shaking.

This is bad . . . bad . . . bad.

They hadn't seen me yet! They were too busy looking for Flubber. As fast and as hard as I could, I bashed into Smith's head from behind.

OUCH . . .

78

I think it hurt me more than him. And now they had seen me.

BANG!!!   **BANG!!!**   **BANG!!!**

Both bad guys were smashing up the lab!

I couldn't let them get Flubber. I couldn't. These guys may have been big, but I'm smart. . . . Suddenly . . .

SMASH!!!!

My screen shattered. . . . *ouch* . . . I was blind. I couldn't see. . . . I spun around . . . and around . . . and *bang!*

HELP!!!

I fell to the ground.

They kept hitting me, . . . banging and bashing my eye, my screen. . . . I could hear Flubber screaming, but there was nothing I could do . . . nothing I could do. Nothing . . . I . . . could . . . do . . . could . . . do.

The light was fading
into darkness. . . .

Everything was going black. . . .

Everything *is* black. . . .

Now I am dreaming. The Professor and Sara are flying through the sky with a check for five million dollars after having successfully sold the Flubber formula to Walter Beeker. They are coming home.

They are so happy!!

I can hear Webber cleaning up
the broken glass.

And now I hear footsteps.
Familiar footsteps. My Professor's
arms are around me, and something is wet. . . . Is it water from
his eyes? Or is my battery leaking?

I am dying. They have killed me. I must give my Professor the EMERGENCY WEEBETTE FILE.

STORK . . . STORK . . . STORK . . . STORK . . . STORK.

Everything is quiet now.

stork \stork\ *n.* a long-legged bird associated with the arrival of a baby, as carried in a bundle by a stork's beak.

MOVIE SECRETS

In real life the actors portraying the bad guys are nice. Neither of them liked killing WEEBO. When Robin Williams, the Professor, filmed WEEBO's dying scene, he was genuinely sad.

The Professor and Sara stormed out of the house and flew straight to Hoenicker's mansion. The Professor was well prepared. He clutched a water pistol and had Flubber tacks in his shoes.

Sara also had tacks, but she carried no pistol.

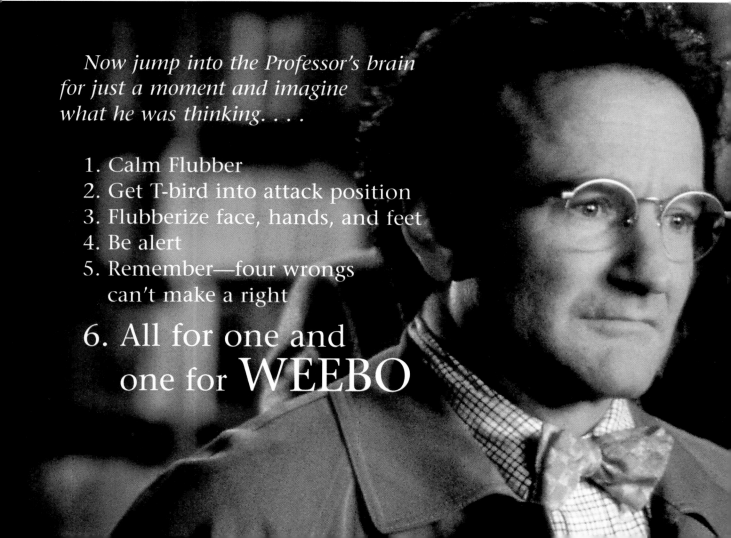

Now jump into the Professor's brain for just a moment and imagine what he was thinking. . . .

1. Calm Flubber
2. Get T-bird into attack position
3. Flubberize face, hands, and feet
4. Be alert
5. Remember—four wrongs can't make a right
6. All for one and one for WEEBO

Hoenicker and his men, including Professor Wilson, were expecting them—but not the fight.

BANG . . .
THUMP . . . SWACK . . . **OUCH!!**
PING . . . **SWING . . .**

Flubber flew into Wilson's mouth— **SWACK!**

GULP!!

And out his bottom!

Scientific Fact:
Four wrongs never make a right.

A VICTORY!! A TRIUMPH!!

The battle was won, but Weebo was lost.

Back at home, the Professor searched his absentminded brain for my final message. But he couldn't remember, . . . so Sara kissed him, . . . which sent love signals into his brain. . . .

love = inspiration!

And he remembered:

STORK!

The Professor opened the STORK file on our main computer. There he found my full and complete design for a new and improved WEEBO.

The Professor called her WEEBETTE.

I designed Weebette in case anything ever happened to me. The Professor didn't remember how I was made, so I started with the basic design and then improved my minor flaws! She is my daughter, and I know she will care for him.

I made some practical changes. . . .

But the most important change that I made was personal. . . .

WEEBETTE is not in love with my Professor. She loves the Professor, Sara, Webber, *and* Flubber.

She has two eyes and a larger screen—from which she transmitted the fourth and final wedding from the church, with Sara, . . .

MOVIE SECRETS Only one WEEBETTE was made.

. . . to the Professor, who remembered
to remember, in his lab.

And everyone flew happily ever after.
THE END.

WEEBO INTERVIEWS ROBIN WILLIAMS

Weebo: What do you love most about me?
RW: I love your brain and the way you are.

Weebo: If you, in real life, could fly in a Flubber car, where would you go?
RW: I would follow an eagle.

Weebo: Would you be afraid?
RW: No, I'm not afraid of flying. I'm afraid of falling!

Weebo: Who would you choose to be stranded on a desert island with, me (WEEBO), Flubber, or Webber?
RW: You (WEEBO), without a doubt!

Weebo: Why?
RW: Because you are interactive. I could stay in touch with the world, even plug into the Library of Congress! If Flubber were there, I would have to be careful not to throw him very hard!

Weebo: If, in real life, you had a ball of Flubber, what would you do with it?
RW: I would Flubberize a room at home by covering all the walls with foam, then I would set it off!

Weebo: What is your favorite scientific fact?

RW: I like Buckyballs and superfluids. Science is like magic!

Weebo: What don't you like about science?

RW: I don't like dissection.

Weebo: Would you like to have me (WEEBO) at home with you in real life?

RW: Yes, for a little while. But I might get bored with your judgment. Although I love your sarcasm!

Weebo: Do you like gadgets in real life?

RW: Yes, I do, very much. I like my computer and playing on the Internet with people all over the world. I like playing the interactive games; it makes me laugh, but if I laugh too much, and I'm not careful, I get killed!

Weebo: What does it feel like to have hair?

RW: Oh, do you want to have hair? I had no idea. I am sorry I didn't give you hair. I think you are lovely just the way you are.

WEEBO INTERVIEWS THE DIRECTOR OF FLUBBER, LES MAYFIELD

Weebo: If you could be Flubber, me, or Webber, who would you be, and why?

LM: I would be Flubber, because he is such a good dancer.

Weebo: Why is Flubber green?

LM: Flubber is fluorescent green because he is such a show-off!

Weebo: If you had a bucket of Flubber, what would you do with it?

LM: I would get a part-time job with the Chicago Bulls and fly like Jordan!

Weebo: How does it feel to be the first director to direct something undirectable?

LM: Flubber was actually quite directable and moldable and lovable.